P9-BZU-196

THE FARM BOOK

STORY AND PICTURES BY E. BOYD SMITH

INTRODUCTION BY BARBARA BADER

HOUGHTON MIFFLIN COMPANY
BOSTON

Library of Congress Cataloging-in-Publication Data

Smith, E. Boyd (Elmer Boyd), 1860–1943.
The farm book.
Summary: Bob and Betty learn about life and work on the farm during a summer vacation they spend with their Uncle John and Cousin Reuben.
ISBN 0-395-32951-5
[1. Farm life—Fiction] I. Title. II. Title: Bob and Betty visit Uncle John.
PZ7.S6465Far 1982 82-12021
[Fic]

Printed in the United States of America

RNF ISBN 0-395-32951-5
PAP ISBN 0-395-54951-5

HOR 10 9 8 7 6 5 4 3

INTRODUCTION

In 1910, when cities meant excitement and progress, while farming was for "hayseeds," a Brooklyn children's librarian named Clara Hunt hailed Houghton Mifflin for bringing out a book that would teach children respect for what the farmer did and show them the satisfaction of doing things for themselves. Indeed, Miss Hunt herself had agitated for the "radical change in juveniles"—from the fanciful to the "honest and true"—which (in the words of the 1910 Houghton Mifflin catalogue) the book represented.

Today *The Farm Book* is a unique pictorial record of a bygone, envied way of life—a round of shared labor and shared pleasure, a chain of production from sowing seed to baking bread. It stands at the head of a long line of distinctively American picture books about the work that people do. And, as the first E. Boyd Smith picture book to be republished, it reintroduces the work of a notable creative personality.

E. Boyd Smith was born in St. John, New Brunswick, in 1860. He was raised in Boston, lived for many years in France, traveled through the West, settled in Wilton, Connecticut, and died there in 1943—the illustrator of more than seventy books for children and adults.

During his years in France, Smith spent the summers outside Paris in little Valombre, whose everyday life, "with all its good and bad, its lights and shadows," he celebrated in *My Village* (1896). There, he draws the villagers, reaping and tying and stacking grain, with a vigor and precision that gives weight to each gesture. He speaks of them in the sly, grave, almost courtly manner that would be a hallmark, later, of his writing for children. Whatever his subject or his audience, Smith didn't sentimentalize or condescend.

In France or in America, Smith could not have escaped the picture books of Maurice Boutet de Monvel—*Jeanne d'Arc,* the most renowned, came out in 1896. Long, flat "albums," printed by the new three- or four-color lithographic process, they combined delicate, subtle colorations with clear definition, striking details, and (sometimes) complex, dramatic composition.

It was a mode of illustration calculated for reproduction and well suited to children. And it appeared at a time when the aesthetic movement (William Morris, Walter Crane), coupled with the burgeoning children's library movement, had created a demand for beautiful children's books. With his first two picture books, *The Story of Noah's Ark* (1905) and *The Story of Pocahontas and Captain John Smith* (1906), Smith established himself as the foremost American in the field.

The Farm Book reflects its diverse origins and transcends them—to convey to children (as a wise librarian, Anne Thaxter Eaton, later wrote) "the adventure to be found in everyday things."

City-bred Bob and Betty, impeccably attired, come to stay at Uncle John's farm. At first they are observers—but not for long. Sundown finds them proudly riding the two farm horses back to the barn. The next day, jackets shed, they will help to plant the corn.

Each day thereafter brings forth discoveries and treats. The chicken yard—and new broods of chicks. A hunt for eggs hidden in the barns. Expeditions to gather wildflowers or fish for minnows. The cows munching grass. The milking: "a never-ending source of interest and mystery to the children."

From corner to corner, the pictures are to pore over. Bob and Betty go with Mike, the hired man, to deliver cans of milk to the train. The engineer gesticulates impatiently, while Mike calmly unloads the cans and jokes with the train hands—and Cousin Reuben holds the restive horses, the dog lolls in the shade under the wagon, other wagons wait at the railroad crossing . . . and Bob and Betty squirm about to take in the whole scene.

Informatively detailed and infectiously enthusiastic, *The Farm Book* was still a favorite of children, Miss Eaton noted, when Smith died in 1943. It is no less tempting now, with its glowing panoramas of old New England and its promise of a ride on the hay wagon, or a trip to the grist mill, at the turn of a page.

Barbara Bader
New York, New York, 1982

PLOWING

It had seemed so long to wait for Spring. But at last it came; and Bob and Betty were taken to the country, for the promised visit to their Uncle John.

The Spring had come early this year, and the air was full of life and promise again. The bluebirds and robins were back once more from their long travels. The squirrels were chattering in the trees, leaping from branch to branch in their jerky way. And even the woodchuck had come out of his hole, to stretch himself after his long sleep. Down in the barnyard the cock crowed loud and shrill, and the hens were nervously bustling about anxious to "set" and hatch out broods of spring chicks. And the long winter with its snow and ice was in a fair way to be soon forgotten.

And now the plowing season began in earnest. Farmer Brown with his two great horses, Sam and Ned, had been at work for hours before the children were awake. Once up, they hurried through their breakfast, and were off and away to the fields to watch the work.

"Gee! Sam! Get up, Ned!" they heard the farmer calling to his horses.

Over the level field, up the slope, came the tugging team, turning up the rich warm soil in good deep furrows, preparing the ground for the sowing which was soon to follow. Across the hill, around through the old apple trees, and down again to the low field, steadily trudged the great horses, turning furrow beside furrow, too many for the children to count, even though they had just come from school. After the field was all plowed the harrow took the place of the plow, and again the team tramped over the same ground, breaking up the clods of earth till all was smooth and fine, ready to receive the seed.

"I'll sow that field to oats," Farmer Brown explained to Bob and Betty.

The children were keenly interested, for though of course they knew what oats were, they had never known anything about where they had come from.

The sun was setting when they started back for the farmhouse. The farmer put the little girl up on big Ned's broad back, and the boy on Sam's, for their first horseback ride.

How proud they were, and what a fine world it was at Uncle John's! That night of course they both felt sure that there was nothing in the whole world like a farmer's life.

SOWING THE SEED

The next morning they had their Cousin Reuben wake them early, so that they should not miss anything.

The day broke bright and warm. The tender leaves on the fruit trees were opening out fast as though in a great hurry to grow and cover up the bare branches.

The farmer was soon at work sowing his field. With a long stately stride he paced up and down, back and forth, scattering the seed with a broad sweeping swing of his arm. When the seed was sown, Sam and Ned were hitched to the brush harrow. This was made of four or five small cedar trees firmly attached to a crosspiece. The harrow was slowly dragged over every part of the field, mixing the seed and earth together, and pressing it well into the ground. And so the planting was completed.

And now the seed, lying in the dark, in the warm moist ground, would slowly germinate, and strike down roots into the soil, and push up green

shoots through the earth into the air, and in good time become a field of ripe waving oats, all ready for the harvester's scythe.

While the farmer was sowing, close by, Mike, the hired man, was marking off a field for corn, with one of the horses harnessed to the corn marker, a sort of wooden plow with three teeth set well apart. With this he marked out straight lines across the field, then turned and crossed them at right angles with more lines. The corn was to be sowed at each point where the lines crossed, so that it would all grow in hills just the same distance apart, with straight lanes between, where the "cultivator" could pass later.

Mike explained all this to the children as he worked, and they enthusiastically began to sow the corn. While Bob, with the long hoe, dug a shallow hole just at the crossing of the lines, Betty dropped in the seed. This was their first attempt at farming, and they found it great fun. They did not then know, as they learned later, that this corn they sowed would grow so tall and dense that they might almost get lost in the midst of it. And often afterwards they had great sport playing "follow my leader" and "hide and seek," among the tall stalks and broad green leaves, when the silk-laden ears of corn were ripening.

DOWN IN THE CHICKEN YARD

With Reuben as guide the children went on voyages of discovery through the great barns and outbuildings. And every day was like a picnic, everything was so new and interesting to them. The old well with its great "sweep" and oaken bucket was a never-failing source of fascination, and it would be hard to keep count of the number of times they drank from it the first few days, just for the fun of lowering the bucket and hoisting it up again.

But the most exciting treat just now was visiting the chicken yard, for this was the time the hens were "setting," and there was of course great excitement in anticipation of the broods of chicks which were expected. And when they did come, pretty downy little things, the children were never weary of watching them, especially as almost each new day brought forth more broods; and even little ducks, funny wobbly creatures, already taking their drinking bowl as a swimming pond.

The geese and turkey-gobbler were not sure that they liked so many children about, but then that didn't matter, nobody minded them.

After playing with the ducks and chickens, the next amusement was gathering the eggs in the hen house. Each nest was visited, though the hens protested. And goodly baskets of eggs were brought in.

Reuben's mother said she thought some of the hens were laying astray, hiding their nests, for they often do this when they want to "set." So she suggested to the children that they hunt through the barns and try to find the missing eggs.

They welcomed the idea with pleasure, for this promised to be more exciting fun than watching the chickens. Off they scampered for the big barn. Here they climbed about in the hay, Reuben, being more used to it than Bob and Betty, boldly showing the way. Betty felt rather timid as the loose hay would slide with her down toward mysterious corners, and there were so many corners and dark holes in the barn. But as Bob and Reuben were doing the same and shouting gleefully, she soon enjoyed the fun. One after the other would triumphantly cry out upon finding a nest. And occasionally a startled hen would rush off with a wild squawk of alarm.

MILKING

Each day brought new interests. New plantings were being made in the fields and vegetable gardens, and our children were learning all about how to be farmers.

They rambled on exploring expeditions over the country, gathered wild flowers in the woods and fields and on the hills, fished with bent pins for minnows in the brooks, and had a good time generally. Tired but happy at night, they were up early the next morning to begin all over again.

One of their favorite jaunts was out to the pasture where the cows were browsing. They could stand for hours and watch them comfortably chewing the cud. At first they felt rather timid toward these great creatures with their fierce-looking horns, but soon learned that they were quite gentle, and even got to know them all by name — Bossy, Daisy, Flossy, and so on.

Bob and Betty used to wonder what the cows were thinking about, for they looked so wise and serious while slowly munching the grass. Reuben assured

J. W. B.

them that they didn't think about anything. But then Reuben may have been mistaken, who knows?

The children often went with Reuben to bring the cows home for milking. The bars were let down, and with little trouble the herd started for the barn. They were so used to this that when it was time for them to be milked and no one came, they would stand by the bars and low, calling for someone to come and open the gate. They couldn't be hurried much and always took time to browse on any choice piece of green along the way.

When they reached the barn they knew the way to the racks, and each cow took her place, some even always choosing the same rack every day. The slats were set in place, holding them from moving about, and the milking began, always a never-ending source of interest and mystery to the children.

The cows "gave down" quart after quart of good warm milk, which was passed through the strainers into the big cans, all waiting brightly cleaned. The farmer, or one of his men, with his low stool passed along from cow to cow till all were milked. Then they were given a good supper of meal, and again turned out to pasture for the night.

SENDING THE MILK TO TOWN

Then the milk was got ready to be sent to town, for each day the farmer shipped it off by the train, to the people who live so far away from cows and green pastures, to the land of the milkman.

Part of the milk was put in the bottles which city people know, while the rest was to be shipped in the big cans. While it was cooling Mike hitched up his team. The children wanted to go with him to the train.

"Come along," he invited, and they climbed into the high seat.

Now Mike always took time to talk and joke with the neighbors along the way, and often came very near being late. He would whip up his horses and go scampering down the long hill to the station as the train rounded the curve and came rumbling in. After all the other farmers had got their milk well loaded on the cars he would arrive just in time to back up to the other side of the train, and while the engineer impatiently shouted for him to hurry up he still would joke with the train hands. Yet he always managed to get the milk off.

With a toot! toot! of warning the train went hurrying on to the next station to gather up more milk, its long streamer of smoke floating behind. From the top of the hill, as they drove home, the children could see it winding its way down the valley.

The next morning the milk would be in the great cities and towns, for sale at the grocery stores, and delivered at the doors. The milkman, before daybreak, would get it from the cars and make his rounds — to the stores, where people through the day could come and buy, and also from house to house, leaving the bottles on the doorsteps, while inside little girls and boys were still fast asleep. When they did wake up and come to the table to have their breakfasts, they drank this nice fresh milk without ever knowing where it came from.

And far away in the country Farmer Brown's cows were calmly grazing in their green meadow, making more milk for tomorrow's breakfast.

And sleek pussy cats too never even dreamed of what they owe to these cows.

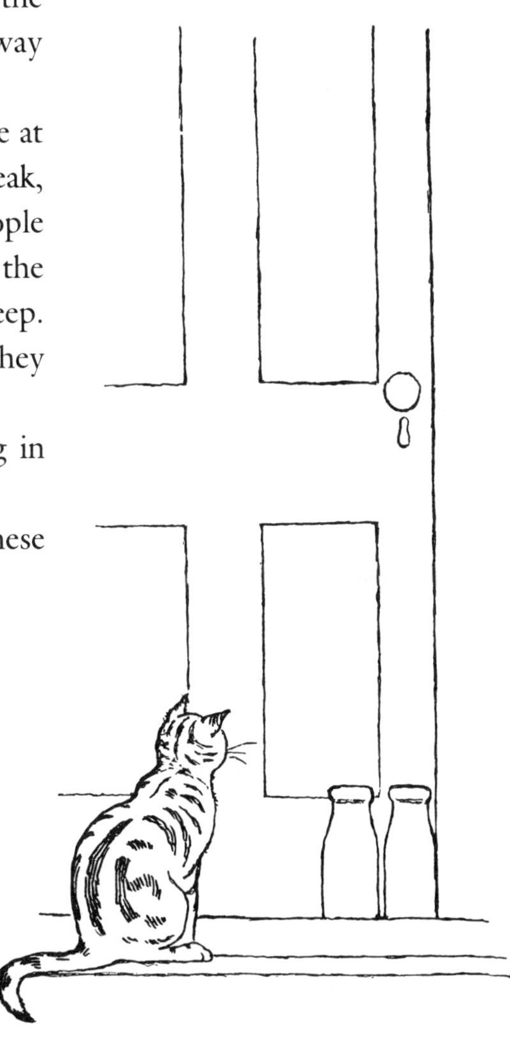

THE DAIRY

Everything was now growing fast. In the vegetable garden the onions and beets and carrots and beans, and ever so many other things, were well started. Reuben showed Bob and Betty how to weed so that they too could help, for on a farm everybody has to work, there are always so many things to be looked after and done all at the same time. The men were busy with the hoe and rake among the long straight rows of vegetables, or out in the fields with the horse cultivator, loosening up the soil to keep it moist, and check the weeds from getting a start, for the weeds will grow even faster than the vegetables, if they get a chance. And everywhere was busy bustle and promise of good crops.

And the sun was so bright and the air so clear and sweet scented, and the birds so lively and cheerfully singing that the two children wondered why everyone didn't live on a farm, and be a farmer. They had already quite made up their minds that that was what they would do when they were grown up.

The clean and orderly dairy always had a charm for them, especially on but-

ter-making days. Here they saw just how it was all done, how the good golden butter was made from the cream, and finally stamped into "pats" or pound "bricks," all ready for the market. And how the cheeses were made in their odd-looking presses. Betty learned to churn. Ella, the "help," another farmer's daughter, did the main churning, and showed her how.

The buttermilk pitcher, always ready, easily and frequently attracted the boys. And a good drink of fresh buttermilk is really worthwhile.

Though the children had always eaten butter at home, they had never given a thought as to where it came from nor how it was made, and now it became so much more interesting to them as they learned all about it — the cows, the milk, the cream, the churning, and then the finished butter. How they would explain all this to their friends when they got back to town! Oh, there was no end of interesting things done on a farm.

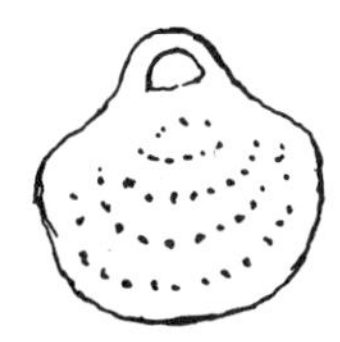

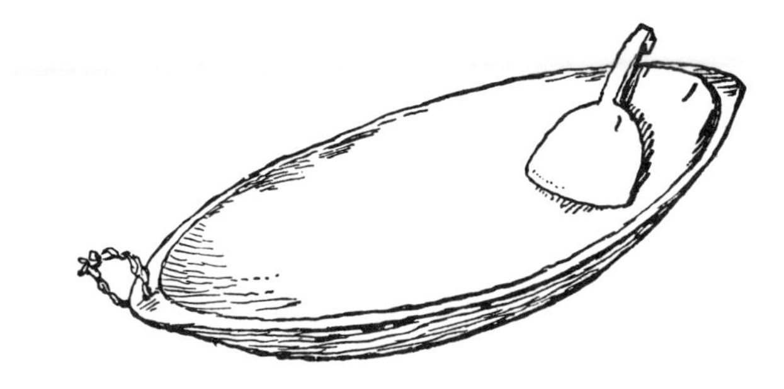

IN THE GARRET

On rainy days, which the farmers always welcomed, for the growing crops needed the rain to make them strong, the children had to amuse themselves indoors.

They always had the big barns to play in, and the hunt for hens' nests. But the favorite rainy-day resort was the great garret. Here were stowed the odds and ends of perhaps nearly a hundred years. And great surprises were to be found in the old boxes and trunks. They dragged out old costumes of Farmer Brown's grandfathers and grandmothers, big hats and coats which looked very funny today, and great wide, furbelowed dresses and beflowered bonnets.

Bob and Betty had great larks dressing up in these old garments and masquerading about, playing old-fashioned men and women with Ella and Rover as audience, while the cat visited the holes and corners in search of possible mice.

Just outside the window they accidentally discovered a bird's nest, with the mother bird on her eggs. It was snugly placed among the branches of a tall cedar tree which grew quite close to the house.

Through long busy days the two birds flying back and forth had worked to build their nest, bringing the material in their bills. When all was safe and strong the mother bird had laid her eggs, and was now "sitting" to hatch out her brood of little birds.

The children were greatly interested and tried to look round the corner without disturbing the birds. But the cat was less discreet and vigorously tried to get through the glass to catch them. The father bird flew off in alarm, but the mother, feeling that her position was safe, still stuck to her post.

And now, though it rained all day, the children found plenty of play and interest between the garret treasures and the bird's nest, not to speak of trips out to the barn to see the cows and the milking. Dodging the showers, under the big family umbrella, too, had its attraction, savoring of real adventure.

HARVESTING

When summer was in its full strength, with green trees and yellow grain, the harvesting season came on. First the hay was to be got in while the weather was good and dry. In the larger fields the reaping machine was working, in others men were mowing, vigorously swinging their long sharp scythes.

The newly cut hay was spread out, and turned from time to time, to get it thoroughly dry, then loaded on the great wagons. As one might easily guess, the children found it the natural thing to dive and roll in this new-cut, sweet-smelling hay. But the greatest fun were the "hayrides." The farmer or his men put them up on top of the high loads, warning them to be careful and hold on. And then away they started, lumbering heavily across the uneven fields, up and down, with many an uneasy jolt.

And from their high perch the world looked so different, and big, to the children, as with fear and joy mixed they held fast while the great load swayed along toward the big barn.

To go through the doors they had to duck down so as not to be scraped off. Once inside, the load was tossed onto the haymows. Then away they went off again to the fields for another load.

Toward the last of the "haying" the first field of ripe wheat was cut — "cradled," as the farmers say, the "cradle" being a sort of framework attached to the scythe, to catch and hold the new-cut grain so that it could be laid in neat rows, without breaking the straw. This was much harder work than mowing the hay with the clean, thin scythe, for the cradle made the wheat scythe heavy and harder to swing.

This wheat, Uncle John explained, had been sowed last fall, just in the same way as they had seen him sow the oats. He told them that this was what bread was made from, and that by-and-by he would take it to the mill to be ground into flour. Oh, yes, he would take them along.

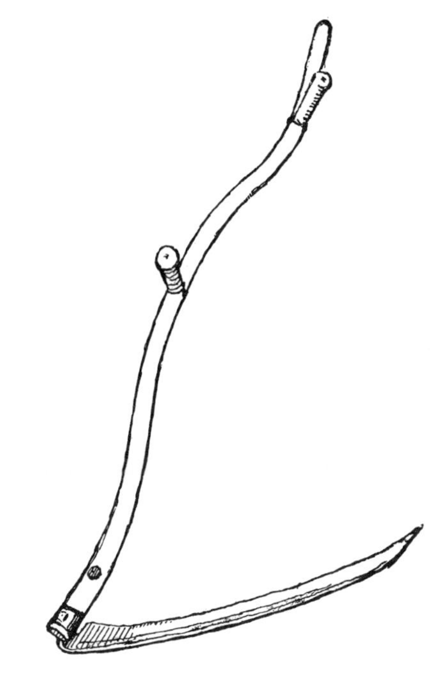

THE GRISTMILL

Some time later, when haying was over, Farmer Brown had some of the wheat threshed with the old-fashioned flail. Though the main crop, when he raised much wheat, was threshed by the threshing machine, the flail answered for small quantities.

The cut grain was spread in heaps on the barn floor, then the farmer or Mike beat it with the heavy flail, separating the grain from the husk.

The next day, with a few bags of this grain they started off for the old gristmill, the children being taken, as promised. The road was long and winding, up hill and down dale, for this is a hilly country. At last, deep down at the foot of a long hill they came to the dingy old mill. It had seen better days, for now the farmers came less and less. Times and methods were changing. They were getting into the habit of selling their grain in town and buying their flour.

In spite of this, the miller was jolly and round, as all millers ought to be. Though the children could not understand the machinery of the mill, he explained to them that the grain was ground into flour between two millstones.

And when the work was done they saw it as flour turned into the bags from which it had come as grain.

Though this was interesting, the great attraction was the water wheel rolling over as the stream poured down upon it, it had such a powerful, persistent, resistless look. This wheel was the power that made the machinery go for grinding the grain. The miller told them that they couldn't find very many of these old wheels nowadays, as the steam mills were steadily driving them out of business.

When they had got back home again to the farm, the farmer's wife began to make bread of the new flour, and, after mixing, kneading, and rising, it was put in the oven to bake, and at last came out in good brown loaves of sweet-smelling bread.

"And now," she said to the children, "you have seen the whole process of making bread — the sowing of the seed, the grain ripening, then the cutting, threshing, and grinding into flour, and now the baking, and here is the bread. Just try a thick slice with fresh butter."

And the children, with ever-ready appetites, tried it, and found it very good.

GOING TO MARKET

Once a week, sometimes oftener, the vegetables, fruits, butter, and other farm products were taken to market.

The day before market day everybody worked busily getting together the things needed for the morrow's load. Even the children, now feeling quite like real workers, did their share and learned to gather beans.

The next morning bright and early the farm was alive with bustle and hurry. The farmer loaded up his big wagon until it couldn't hold any more. There were boxes of berries and baskets of peaches, with tomatoes and beets and vegetables of every kind, from the beans Bob and Betty had picked to big round cabbages and rich juicy melons. Chickens and eggs were a part of the load as well.

The horses were cleaned and groomed, the wagon and harnesses well washed, and everything made to look neat and trim.

The white canvas wagon top was put in place, to protect everything from the sun. The children climbed into their seats, though they really had taken their places long before the others were ready. Reuben brought the lunch basket,

and, with Rover proudly leading the way, they started for the town, to sell what the farm had produced and buy what it needed.

Along the road other wagons of all sizes and kinds joined them, each with its load of garden "truck," and even here and there a pig shrilly protesting against the whole proceeding.

When they reached the town the streets were already filling, and everybody struggling for the best places, and the marketing was going on in a lively way.

The children enjoyed the confusion and excitement of all the selling and buying. And the sight of such quantities of vegetables astonished them, for they had never imagined there were so many in the world.

After Uncle John had disposed of his load, visits to the different stores were made for shopping, for town supplies were needed on the farm, and new tools to be bought. And all in all it was a memorable day for the children, and that night they dreamed of heaps of cabbages and stacks of spades all dancing cheerfully together.

SUNDAY

Sunday came as a much needed day of rest on the farm, after the busy week's work, and everybody arose later that day. It opened so quietly, without the usual early farm noises and activities, that to the children it seemed like a different day from all the others. And of course it was, for though the stock had to be watered, the chickens fed, and the cows milked, the farm work stopped, and all was very quiet.

After breakfast preparations began for going to church, with much getting ready, shining of boots and shoes, and general dressing up.

On all the farms Sunday clothes were being donned, and teams "hitched up."

Across the fields came the slow, sober ringing of the church bells, reminding the farmers that it was time to come. From every direction they now came trailing in to the church green, in carriages or wagons, or on foot, as might be. The horses, without unharnessing, were hitched in the long sheds behind the church, where farmers meeting were talking over the events of the week. For Sunday is a great day for the country people to get together and discuss the news, as well as attend service.

Everything was quiet and orderly, for though Sunday in New England is an important day, it is a calm one.

Already summer had gone and the trees were turning gold or crimson, and the country was wonderfully beautiful on this bright autumn day.

Bob and Betty made many new acquaintances at church and got to know the neighbors' girls and boys, and visits to their homes were added to the already long list of pleasures and experiences.

Sunday was especially a day for visiting, and family parties made things cheerful in many homes.

Sometimes the children's parents would come to spend the weekend, and Bob and Betty would proudly show the sights, and explain things, for now they knew all about it. Down in the meadow the big horses, Sam and Ned, wondered, if they ever do wonder, how it was that they had such an easy time today. The cows grazed peacefully as usual, curiously following the visitors with their big soft eyes. And even the fields seemed to rest.

WOOD-CUTTING

As the season steadily advanced toward winter, the interest never waned for the children. Though the berry-picking was over, always a source of adventure and fun and bramble scratches, there was still the "nutting" — chestnuts and hickories — with daring tree-climbing, torn clothes, and bruises, but oh, such good times.

And then the great brush fires, the cleaning up of the fields, to be all ready for next year's work, for this year's was nearly over.

Our children had been allowed to stay on a little later than first intended, so that they enjoyed the Hallowe'en larks of the country, such as "bobbing" for apples, telling fortunes, and, best of all, the "jack-o'-lanterns," big pumpkins hollowed out with candles inside.

This year the snow came early, none too early for Bob and Betty, for here were new possibilities for fun.

All the farm work being now well attended to, the men with axes and saws set to work in the woods getting in the winter's supply of firewood, and piling

up "cord" wood for the market. For after all the vegetables have been sold there is always a market for wood. Houses must be warmed in winter.

The three children, all in their stout rubber boots — Farmer Brown called them the rubber-boot brigade — joined the wood choppers. They watched with eager interest the fall of each great tree, as it roared and crashed down through the surrounding branches.

Mike and the other men sawed them in lengths, and the ox team with its wood sled carted the cords off away behind the big barn.

That night — this was to be their last night in the country, for tomorrow they were to go back to town and school — the children sat around the blazing logs of the day's cutting, brightly burning in the old fireplace, and watched the pictures in the flames, laying up more memories to tell about to their friends who had never spent a vacation on a farm.